My Life

Lisa James

I am a frog.
Look at my life.

I am a butterfly.
Look at my life.

eggs

water

A frog comes from an egg.
The egg is in water.

egg

leaf

A butterfly comes from an egg.
The egg is on a leaf.

tadpoles

A tadpole comes out of the egg.
It is very small.

leaf

caterpillars

A caterpillar comes out of the egg.
It is very small.

legs

The tadpole grows legs.
It grows bigger and bigger.

flower

The caterpillar eats and eats.
It grows bigger and bigger.

tail

froglet

The tadpole grows into a froglet.
The froglet has a tail.

The caterpillar grows a chrysalis.
The caterpillar rests in the chrysalis.

The froglet grows into a frog.
It has no tail.

The chrysalis opens.
It is a butterfly!

A Frog's Life

eggs

tadpole with legs

froglet

frog

The frog lays eggs.
This is my life!

A Butterfly's Life

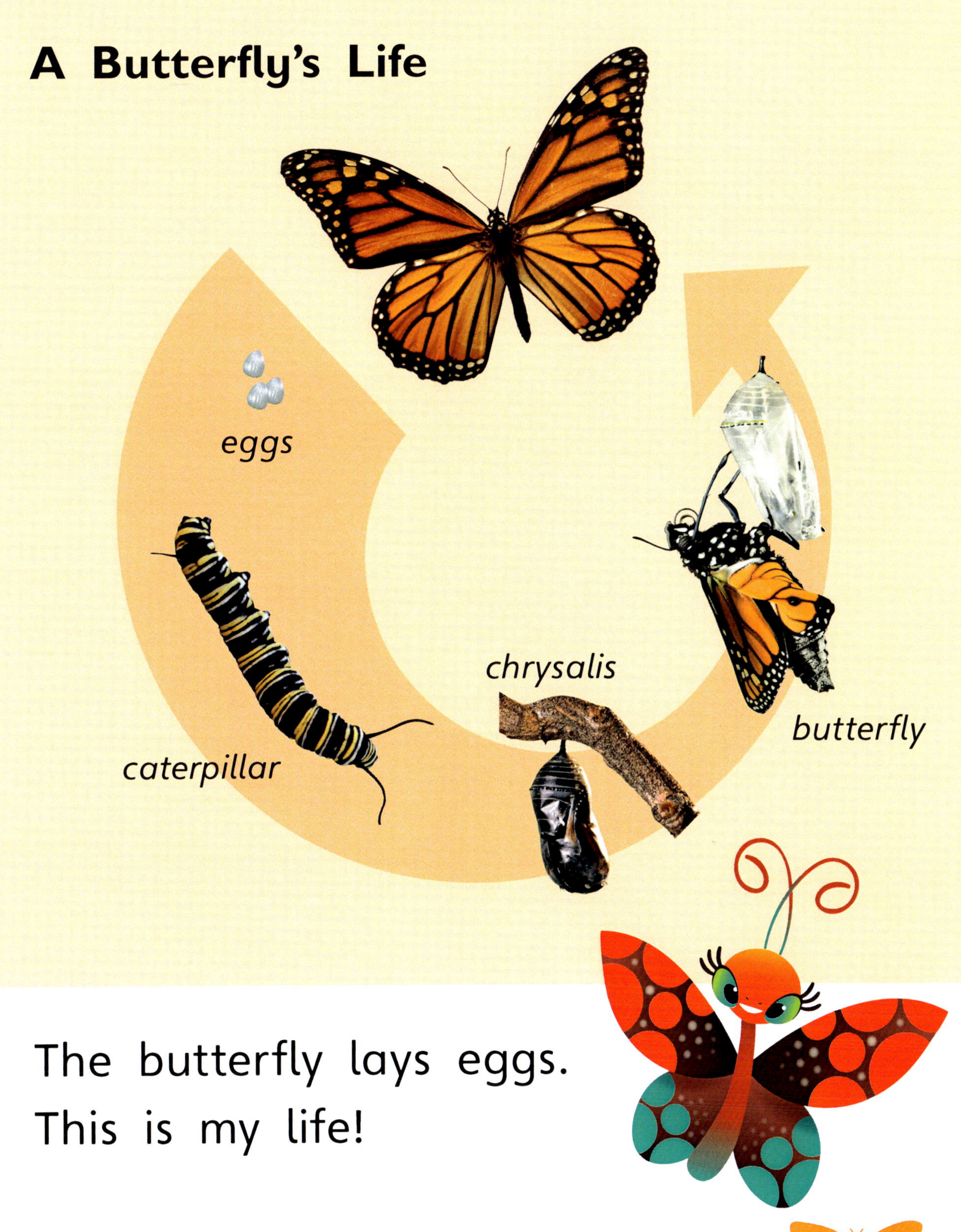

The butterfly lays eggs.
This is my life!

Picture Index

Frog

Butterfly